The Tree that Came Home

An IslandWood Story

Inspired by the true story of a 92-foot beam
that returned to Bainbridge Island, Washington.

Written by IslandWood Founder, Debbi Brainerd,
with contributions from many others.

Illustrated by Katherine Zecca

ISLANDWOOD™
A School in The Woods

Dedicated to children everywhere
in whose hearts and hands
the future rests.

CHAPTERS

Additional Resources

Most people think that trees do not talk or have stories to tell. But maybe— just maybe—they do.

If you cross the cold, gray waters of Puget Sound to Bainbridge Island, you'll find a school in the woods called IslandWood.

And if you join the students there at sunset as they gather around a crackling campfire, you might hear one of their favorite stories—a story with deep roots not far from you.

The night the
EARTH SHOOK

One cold January night in the year 1700, a powerful earthquake shook Bainbridge Island and the entire Puget Sound region.

The trembling ground sent animals scurrying for cover. Falling trees and huge boulders tumbled down mountainsides into bodies of water, causing rivers and bays to flood.

The morning's light revealed widespread devastation across the island.

Thousands of trees had fallen during the night. Some of the oldest ones had been growing in the forest for more than 1,000 years. Their branches no longer shaded the forest floor as they had for so long. Without their shade, large sections of land were bathed in direct sunlight.

Soon the dry, hot months of summer arrived. A lightning storm ignited a rash of forest fires, which were fueled by the fallen trees. Within days, much of the lush green forest had vanished into ashes and clouds of smoke.

Fortunately, a scattering of old trees was still standing.

These giant trees survived because they had grown a thick protective bark at the base of their trunks. Even though their bark was as black as charcoal, it had protected the living wood within.

With the abundant new clearings and the fertile ash from the fires, the area was now perfect to grow a whole new generation of trees.

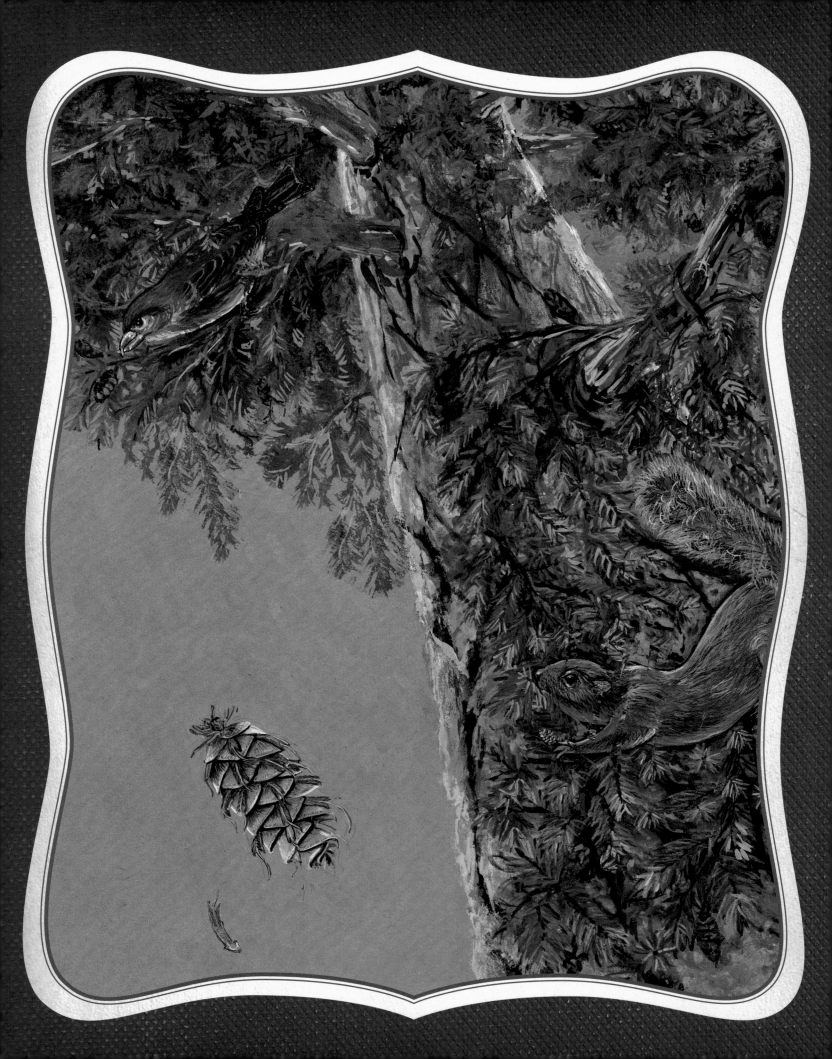

The Special Seed

Autumn arrived in the forest, bringing winds that rustled the branches of the surviving trees.

These old trees held thousands of cones that were ripe with seeds. Red crossbills and flocks of noisy pine siskens flew from branch to branch, plucking the seeds from the cones. Many seeds fell to the forest floor. Some of them were snatched up by the tiny nuthatches and chickadees foraging for food below.

But the busiest forager of all was not a bird.

It was the chickaree, a native squirrel commonly known as the Douglas squirrel. With cold weather soon to come, the chickarees busily gathered fir seeds to store as winter food. They chewed the cones off the trees and then dropped them to the ground, where they tore off the cones' outer scales to reach their favorite seeds inside.

As one enthusiastic squirrel tossed a cone from a giant fir tree, a large, ripe seed sprang from the cone into the air. The seed landed on the ground near the tree from which it had come. Lying there, it looked no different from all the other fallen seeds. It's what would become of this particular seed that would make it quite special.

The seed sank into the soft, moist blanket of duff, where it slept through fall and winter.

When spring arrived, the seed woke from its long hibernation. The forest was quiet, except for the croaks of tree frogs in the distance. "Where am I?" the seed cried out. A deep voice answered from within the earth.

"This is your forest. This is your home."

The small seedling pushed up and out of its shell to learn where the voice had come from. The warm sun cracked the shell open to reveal a root tip inside. The massive tree continued in its deep strong voice, "You are fortunate to be alive, little one. Most of your siblings did not survive the long, wet winter."

Cradled in the shadow of the tree's enormous branches, the seedling asked, "Who am I? How did I get here?"

"Your name is Douglas," replied the tree. "Every autumn, I produce thousands of cones that ripen with seeds and drop to the ground. Many of them are eaten by hungry animals. Others drown in the rain.

"But you were strong, Douglas. You survived."

That spring, Douglas learned more about the beginnings of his life from his parent tree and the animals that roamed the hillside. When summer arrived and warmed him, his tiny taproot stretched down into the soil, searching for moisture and nourishment. Once he was firmly anchored in the earth, his stem opened to reveal his tiny needles to the light, and he began his life's most important work—photosynthesis. His new needles would use the sun's energy to make the food needed to support his growth.

Each day, Douglas continued to reach for the sun.

Perhaps one day he would grow as tall as his parent tree, which towered above him and reached more than 200 feet into the sky. At the moment, the likelihood seemed very remote.

Douglas was only one and a half inches tall.

By the spring of his third year, Douglas stood nine inches tall—almost the height of the raccoons that ambled by. On the hillside around him, trilliums bloomed and sword ferns unfolded. Mushrooms seemed to pop up overnight. Banana slugs inched by, leaving shiny slime trails in their path. Paper-thin orange bark curled off the trunk of a big Madrone tree that had survived the fire.

His forest community was beginning to feel like home.

Early one morning, as he bathed in drops of dew that fell from the trees around him, a noise rose in the distance. Something was tearing young plants from the ground, and it was moving closer to Douglas.

Two black-tailed deer emerged through the darkness. Stepping gracefully over fallen trees, they lowered their heads to nibble on the tender tops of young seedlings. Douglas was still as one of the deer stepped toward him. Would he be the deer's next bite of breakfast?

Suddenly, a crow swooped in from above and called loudly as it landed on the branch of the nearby Madrone tree. The deer raised their heads and paused, frozen in place like statues.

The bird's cry attracted other crows, which joined in the raucous calls. Startled, the deer bounded off through the woods to find quieter ground for grazing. Douglas was safe for now. But there would always be hungry deer in the forest.

Foraging deer were not the only danger to a young sapling.

In his sixth winter, Douglas weathered the worst storm of his young life. Fierce winds gusted up to eighty miles an hour. Large tree limbs creaked. Branches broke. Leaves and needles flew through the air. The thick upper branches of the older trees gave him some protection, but several of the saplings around him were crushed by fallen limbs. Torrents of rain continued through the night, and seedlings that had made their homes on lower ground drowned in standing pools of water.

Douglas was fortunate to have taken root on top of the hill. Once he absorbed all the water he needed, the excess rainwater flowed through the soil and down to the harbor below. Finally, the rain and wind subsided.

His roots continued to grow deeper and stronger.

The
WEB OF LIFE

By his twelfth year, Douglas had matured into a healthy sapling. He would not develop cones and seeds for another four years. Yet he was almost three feet tall, and his branches had become a playground for the winter wrens, nuthatches and chickadees.

Most of the birds around him ate berries and seeds. But one summer day, a large bird with a very long beak landed on his parent tree and began eating insects off its bark. It was a great pileated woodpecker. Douglas stood helplessly by as the big redheaded bird pecked a large oval hole in the bark of his parent's trunk with a relentless drumming noise.

"Rat-tat-tat! Rat-tat-tat!"

"Stop!" Douglas said. "You're going to hurt that tree!"

The woodpecker paid no attention. So Douglas used his most powerful voice—one that any bird would understand.

"STOP HURTING MY PARENT!"

The woodpecker stopped its pecking and turned to Douglas. "I can't hurt your parent. The beetles and fungus have already done that!" Staring intently at Douglas, the woodpecker continued, "Bark beetles have bored into the trunk and laid millions of eggs. The larvae and bugs are eating their way through the sapwood now. That's why I'm here. I love to eat those tasty little insects!"

The woodpecker was right. Many of the elder tree's needles had already turned red, and parts of its bark were a pale gray.

Douglas asked his parent, "Will you be all right?"

A soft breeze stirred the branches of the giant fir tree. At last his parent tree spoke. "I am old and growing weaker. Soon I will no longer have the strength to fight off these beetles, and my roots will stop absorbing water. Eventually, I will no longer be able to grip the earth."

"What will happen to you?" Douglas asked.

"I will move on to another part of the web of life," his parent tree answered.

"You see, when we can no longer stand as living trees, our trunks fall to the ground. Over time, we decompose and become food for other plants and trees as well as insects. In fact, my rotting wood could become a nurse log for the seedlings and saplings you produce."

Douglas stood silent and still, taking in his parent's wisdom and the surprising turns that life can take.

"You know Douglas," his parent continued, "everything in our world is interconnected. We all have a reason for being. Even after we die, we continue to have a purpose in the web of life."

Many times in the years ahead, the teachings of his parent would come back to him.

From Storm to Sun

That winter, in the middle of the night, a massive storm blew in from the north. The strong winds caused great stress to Douglas's parent tree. Douglas stood helplessly by, his branches tossed and turned by the powerful gusts.

After hours of strong winds, a rupturing sound emerged from the earth.

The roots of his parent tree slowly surfaced as its huge trunk thundered to the ground.

The next morning, Douglas's parent lay on the forest floor. Small animals were building new homes for themselves under the massive trunk and exposed roots, while others hauled away pieces to furnish their existing homes.

Douglas overlooked the collapse of the tree whose seed had given him life.

His parent had stood growing and taking in nutrients from the soil and air for more than 800 years. Now it would release those same nutrients back into the earth so that the forest community could reuse them. As his parent had taught him, everything was interconnected— and somehow that comforted him on this sad day.

Later that day, Douglas felt the intense heat of the sun.

Without his parent tree to provide shade, Douglas bathed in sunlight all afternoon.

He could now grow more rapidly than the other trees on the hillside.

A girl named
SKUKUOY

Standing tall on the north hillside above the harbor in his sixty-second year, Douglas had become part of a thriving community. River otters played in the nearby stream, and migrating birds flew in and out of the estuary at the end of the harbor. Many birds landed on Douglas's high branches; at 120 feet in height, he was as big as a ten-story building.

One foggy spring morning, at high tide, two long canoes filled with native people entered the harbor.

Upon reaching the shore, they jumped out and pulled their canoes onto the rocky beach. Most of them quickly left the shore and disappeared into the forest.

"Who are those people?" Douglas asked the ancient cedar tree standing nearby.

"They are the Suquamish," the cedar replied. "They are the First People of this land. Their name means 'people of the clear salt water.' They come to our harbor every spring and fall to catch salmon in the stream and dig clams on the shore at low tide. Afterward, they dry them in the sun or cook them in their smokehouse."

This was very different from the way Douglas gathered his food. He stood in the same place, drawing nutrients from the ground, taking in carbon from the air, and using his needles to photosynthesize energy from the sun.

The giant cedar tree spoke again. "The Suquamish also gather roots and berries to store for winter. Sometimes they strip cedar bark and use it to weave baskets, clothing and mats. Once they took some of my bark."

"Did it hurt?" Douglas asked.

"Not really," the cedar replied. "They know to take only a small portion so that I can continue to grow."

The Suquamish quickly built several temporary shelters, where they would sleep that night. They used wooden poles for the frames and attached woven mats made from cattail plants for the walls and roofs.

The next morning, the men and boys carried nets to trap salmon in the freshwater stream that fed the estuary. The women and girls walked into the forest with their baskets.

One young girl gathered salmonberries on the hillside below Douglas.

She placed some of the soft, ripe berries in her basket. But almost as many of them went into her mouth, coloring her lips orange with berry juice. As she picked and ate, the girl walked toward the large salmonberry bush growing close to Douglas. After picking all of the ripe berries on the bush, she wandered over to Douglas and sat down against his trunk to enjoy the coolness of his shade.

Douglas whispered, "That's a fine basket of salmonberries."

Startled, the little girl looked up, listening to the faint murmurs of his branches moving in the wind. "Hello," she responded shyly.

She actually heard him! Douglas had never communicated with a person before. "What's your name?" he asked, with a rustle of his branches.

"My name is Skukuoy (Sue-coy)," the girl replied. "It means 'precious little girl.' I'm nine years old. What's your name, and how old are you?"

"I'm Douglas. I have lived for 62 years. But in the life of a tree, I'm young, like you. My parent tree told me that some of my relatives have lived in our forest for more than 1,000 years."

Skukuoy remembered the stories her father had told her about the ancient cedar trees. "We use old cedar trees for many things back home. My father cuts planks for our long house and carves canoes from giant cedar trees," she said.

Skukuoy looked at him thoughtfully, "My grandmother says that every living thing in our world has a purpose. We use your kind of wood to make spear handles, and we use the pitch from your bark to make our canoes waterproof."

It was good to know that his type of tree had helped Skukuoy's people in such important ways.

Their visit was interrupted by a distant call. "That's my mother," Skukuoy said. As she picked up her basket and ran toward the harbor, she shouted back to Douglas, "Thank you for your shade!"

The following spring, Skukuoy and her family returned to the harbor. She was so excited to show Douglas her new basket that she ran all the way up the hill.

"See!" she said, out of breath, "I made my first cedar basket this winter. Grandmother told me it wasn't woven tight enough, so I had to make three more before I got it right. This basket is my fourth!"

"It's beautiful," Douglas told her. "It looks like it could hold water."

Skukuoy laughed with delight, knowing that this was a big compliment. "My grandmother says that some day, with lots of practice, I will be able to weave a basket that really does hold water. But this one is fine for berries."

True Friendship

Each spring, Skukuoy stopped to visit Douglas after she had filled her basket with berries. Resting against his trunk, she shared stories about her family's home in Suquamish, which was north of Douglas's island.

Sadly, each autumn, it was time again for Skukuoy to say goodbye. Her family filled their canoes with food as they prepared to move back to their permanent home for the winter.

"Douglas," Skukuoy said, standing at the base of his trunk and looking up at his evergreen branches, "I will miss you this winter, but I will see you again in the spring when the salmon turn red and return to the stream to spawn." Running downhill, she turned to look back at him and shouted, "Thank you for being my friend!"

When a bald eagle circled above, they both knew that, as master and protector of the sky, this great bird was blessing their friendship.

Skukuoy reached the shore and climbed into one of the canoes. As her family paddled out of the harbor, she looked up at the hillside and waved to her favorite tree in the forest. Douglas responded by catching one of his highest branches in the wind.

As many summers passed, Skukuoy married and had children of her own. Each year, when the days grew longer and the air warmer, her growing family visited the harbor to gather food and visit Douglas.

One year, the forest suffered a serious drought. Small streams evaporated, preventing salmon from reaching their spawning ground. When plants on the forest floor died, insects became scarce and many birds went hungry. As his parent had told him, everything was interconnected.

Douglas had never before been this thirsty.

He and other conifer trees lost more needles than usual that year. Leaves on deciduous trees curled up and fell to the ground earlier than usual, helping the trees to conserve moisture. The threat of summer fires was high in the forest, which was as dry as a tinderbox.

The arrival of autumn brought back cool weather. Yet still there was no rain. When Skukuoy returned the following spring, she and her children carried baskets of water from the disappearing stream to pour at the base of Douglas. After watering his roots, Skukuoy held up a beautiful, tightly woven basket.

"See!" she proudly announced. "I told you that one day my woven baskets would hold water." Growing serious, she added, "Without the inner bark of the cedar tree, I could not bring you this water."

Each day, Skukuoy's family brought water for him and his saplings. Their thoughtful care kept Douglas alive, but his youngest saplings did not survive because they lacked a well-established root system.

For the next several years, Douglas hardly grew at all.

The arrival of
SHIPS & SETTLERS

At 92 years old and 133 feet, Douglas was so tall that birds nesting in his upper branches could see the snow-capped Cascade Mountains to the east, the sharp ridges of the Olympic Mountains to the west, and the single majestic peak of Mount Rainier to the south.

One spring morning in 1792, a large ship with enormous sails of billowing white canvas rounded the southern end of the island. Unlike the canoes, which were made from one tree, it had taken the wood from a small forest to build this massive ship. Dozens of men scrambled up its rigging to furl its sails.

A huge anchor was dropped into the water, and sailors' voices rang out as they lowered two small boats and rowed to shore.

With axes in hand, several men headed straight for three slender trees along the shoreline and began chopping them down. Wood chips flew, and the trees fell quickly. The men stripped the bark and branches off the tree trunks and took the long, straight poles back to the main ship.

Several days later, Skukuoy brought Douglas big news.

"My family and I met Captain Vancouver! He sailed here from England on his ship called the *Discovery*. On his way here, he got caught in a storm that broke some of the poles that hold his ship's sails. He called them masts. His crew saw the straight trees growing on our island, so they stopped and cut some down to replace their broken masts," she explained. With a smile, she continued. "Douglas—if you were smaller and standing closer to the harbor, you might have become one of those new masts holding up their sails!"

That night, as moonlight shone on the anchored ship, Skukuoy's remark came back to Douglas. What would it be like to travel to a faraway place?

In the morning, a clanging noise echoed throughout the harbor as the *Discovery's* anchor was hauled aboard. It wasn't long before the large ship's white sails were unfurled and filled with wind, carrying Captain Vancouver and his men out of sight.

Change Comes to the Island

At 163 years old, Douglas reached 160 feet into the sky. He had become a landmark for eagles, which perched on his upper limbs to scan the harbor for salmon.

Many ships had sailed past the island since Captain Vancouver had visited almost 71 years ago. In that time, the Industrial Revolution had transformed America. Fifteen presidents had come and gone, from George Washington to the sixteenth president, Abraham Lincoln. The country was embroiled in a bitter Civil War. The world beyond Bainbridge Island was changing.

Douglas's world was about to change, too.

One spring morning in 1863, a ship anchored in the dark gray water just off the island and two men entered the harbor in a small rowboat. One of them was a large bearded man, who repeatedly lowered a long rope with a piece of iron into the water to measure its depth. His name was Captain William Renton, and he was hoping to find a harbor deep enough for ocean-going ships.

A month later, with a down payment of ten dollars, Captain Renton purchased the land around the harbor from the government for $1.25 an acre. He now owned Douglas and thousands of other trees on his new 164-acre property.

Soon, dozens of men and teams of oxen were ferried to the island. The steady rhythm of axes echoed across the water as men chopped down trees near the shore, sawed them into logs, and dragged them away. They stacked smaller branches into huge piles and set them on fire. For months, the dark gray smoke from these fires engulfed the forest and harbor, making it difficult to see.

Large buildings and small houses began to appear down the hillside from Douglas. Some of the biggest logs were thrust into the muddy floor of the harbor, and huge wharfs were built on top of the logs to connect the land to the deeper part of the bay.

While Skukuoy had made her last visit to Douglas and his island many years ago, the younger generations of her family continued to come and collect food each year. But this spring, when her great-great-grandchildren arrived in their canoes and saw the bustling construction around the harbor, they stopped paddling and stared in disbelief at the frenzy of activity.

Without coming ashore, they turned their canoes and paddled away.

The age of
FALLERS, BUCKERS & BULLWHACKERS

By 1890, Douglas overlooked a booming mill operation.

More than 1,000 people lived around the harbor in the young town of Port Blakely. Columns of gray smoke rose high into the air from the heavy boilers and steam engines that powered the new sawmill. The sounds of axes and shouting lumberjacks rang throughout the forest. Teams of oxen pulled freshly cut logs to the crest of the hillside, where the logs were rolled down into the harbor and floated into a gated holding area. Eventually, a huge chain lifted the immense logs out of the water and up to the second floor of the mill, where they were cut. When the logs appeared on the other side of the mill, they had been transformed into lumber.

Once the lumberjacks had cut the largest trees from the nearest hillsides, they began harvesting other parts of the island. Still, they had not visited the hill that was home to Douglas and other trees younger than 300 years. His only visitors were the children from Port Blakely who came up after school to play hide-and-seek around the base of his large trunk.

Most of his news continued to come from the birds that landed on his branches and brought him daily reports of the human activity.

One morning, a great horned owl came to rest after a long night of hunting mice and shrews. Knowing that the owl often had a great deal of information, Douglas asked, "What's going on out there?"

"Those men are chopping down the biggest fir trees in the forest," the owl replied.

"You mean like me?" Douglas asked.

"Well…they are taking only the very oldest trees," the owl said as she nestled into a dark, protected area of Douglas's thick branches for a nap. "They are cutting the old-growth trees that survived the great fire of 1700. Those trees are at least 400 years old. Some have lived nearly 1,000 years. The men aren't interested in trees as young as you."

But Douglas began to stand out in the forest as the older, taller trees were removed. What would happen when the older trees were gone?

After 36 years of operation, the Port Blakely Mill had dramatically changed the landscape around Douglas. The region's giant trees were gone. The settlement around the mill had grown to become one of the largest towns in the Pacific Northwest. Ships from distant parts of the world sailed here to fill their cargo holds with timber.

At 200 years old, Douglas was now the tallest tree overlooking the harbor.

One afternoon, four lumberjacks trudged up his hill. They had canvas bags slung over their shoulders and led a team of oxen carrying heavy equipment. They stopped at the base of Douglas, knocking on his bark and measuring his circumference.

After making a calculation, one man shouted, "He's over six feet in diameter!"

The lumberjacks were soon hard at work clearing a path on the uphill side of Douglas. The fallers axed a notch on either side of his trunk, about four feet from the ground. They inserted wooden planks, called springboards, into the notches and stood on them to reach a higher, narrower portion of trunk.

Once they had chopped a V-shaped wedge into the trunk, the men traded their axes for the wooden handles of a long crosscut saw. With one man on each side, they pulled the long blade back and forth, periodically squirting kerosene on the blade to remove Douglas's sticky pitch from the saw. When a loud cracking noise began, the men jumped from their springboards to the ground.

"T - I - M - B - B - E - R - R - R - R!" roared one of the fallers.

Douglas began to lean as a familiar eagle flew in circles above him. "This is a good omen," he said to himself. "It's my turn to move to another part of the web of life, and my friend the eagle is blessing my transformation."

With a thunderous crash, Douglas fell onto the forest floor, the way his parent tree had fallen so many years before.

"Bring on the buckers!" shouted one of the men. The buckers removed all of his branches and the bullwhackers attached chains to his trunk so the oxen could pull him down to the harbor.

At the end of the day, Douglas rested in the cool salt water.

Douglas
LEAVES HOME

Like so many trees before him, Douglas was to be cut into lumber at the Port Blakely Mill.

His massive trunk was lifted from the mill pond and carried to the doors of the sawmill, where the high-pitched sound of a circular power saw filled the air. Fifteen minutes later, Douglas emerged from the other side of the mill as a spectacular beam of gigantic proportions. He was 92 feet long, two feet square, and weighed over 10,000 pounds.

The mill workers referred to him proudly as a big *Port Blakely toothpick*. Such huge wooden beams could only be made from the largest and straightest trees.

Soon Douglas was moving again. A steam-powered crane picked him up and swung him into the air, lowering him onto two railcars. He was much too big for one. The railcars were rolled onto the wharf and onto a barge waiting in the harbor. That afternoon, a tugboat pulled the timber-filled barge out of the harbor and away from the island that had been home to Douglas for 200 years.

Within an hour, the tugboat and barge reached the busy port of Seattle.

The railcars were quickly unloaded from the barge. As the sun set, a massive black locomotive arrived, hooked up to the railcars, and pulled them north along the Puget Sound shoreline. The train gathered speed as it left the coast and headed east toward the Cascade Mountains. A full moon rose and lit the train's path as it climbed Snoqualmie Pass, then began its descent into eastern Washington.

The next day, as the sun appeared on the horizon, the train braked to a screeching halt at a railroad yard in Butte, Montana. The two railcars that carried Douglas were unhooked from the rest of the train, which traveled on without him.

There were no trees in sight. The barren landscape felt strange and unwelcoming. Where was he?

Later that day, a large metal crane appeared. It lifted Douglas off the train cars and laid him on wooden blocks near a large sign that read: Bell Diamond Mine.

"Say, will you look at that!" one of the miners said to another as they arrived for work. "That wooden beam must be 100 feet long. It's probably a replacement for one of the legs of our broken headframe."

Douglas lay on the blocks for days as the miners came and went. Each morning, they crowded into a metal cage and shut its heavy metal door with a clang. Grinding gears made odd sounds as the cage disappeared, carrying miners down into the mine. All day long, the sounds of drilling and blasting rose from deep underground. The cage returned to the surface, carrying large carts filled with glistening rocks of ore that contained copper, gold and silver. Contrary to its name, the mine did not appear to hold diamonds.

One afternoon, a miner pointed at Douglas as he passed by with a co-worker. "It's a shame we no longer need that giant Port Blakely timber. Since the boss didn't want to lose a single day of work, he had our broken headframe bolted back together."

"Yep," agreed the other miner. "It's a pity to see that huge beam just lying there."

As weeks turned into months, and months into years, Douglas lay under a growing pile of discarded mining equipment. Now that the miners had forgotten him, it

seemed his only purpose was to provide shelter for the countless beetles, ants and other little creatures that lived underneath him.

When the stock market crashed in 1929, many companies went out of business. The Bell Diamond Mine was no different. The people who had once prospered there left in search of new jobs. The winter winds blew snow down the empty mineshaft, and loose shutters flapped against the windows of abandoned buildings.

Douglas had become part of a ghost town.

Welcome to Silver Star

One morning, the quiet around Douglas was disrupted with a series of slams, bangs and thuds.

Piece by piece, hundreds of pounds of metal, junk and wood scraps from the collapsed buildings were lifted off him and thrown to the ground. For the first time in 65 years, the warmth of the brilliant Montana sun reached Douglas.

"Say, what do we have here?" a man shouted.

"Well, I'll be darned!" he continued. "Lucky thing they laid you on these blocks, or you would have rotted. Looks like you're one of those gigantic trees from Washington State!" Scratching his head and gazing at Douglas, he continued, "I'm going to take you home and show you off."

The man climbed into his pick-up and drove off, leaving Douglas in a cloud of dust. When the dust cleared, it revealed weeds covering the train tracks that had brought him here so long ago.

A few hours later, the pickup returned, followed by a larger truck towing a long flatbed trailer. The drivers got out of their trucks and stood scratching their chins as they regarded Douglas.

"I don't know, Lloyd," said one man. "I think you're plumb crazy! This big feller won't fit on my truck, either. Why don't you just cut this old thing up and use it for firewood?"

"Not on your life, Dick," Lloyd said. "He's a real beauty! I think we can stack shorter beams on your flatbed until they're about nine feet off the ground, and then strap this big beam on top of them. He'll hang out the back. But I've got red flags to hang on the end."

It took hours to winch Douglas up onto the flatbed truck and securely tie down all 92 feet of him. He was so long that he extended past the truck and trailer at both ends as they slowly pulled out onto the highway.

A short time later, they reached a road sign that read: Butte, Montana, City Limit.

As they drove through town, people stared in amazement at the giant piece of wood strapped to the flatbed. A sudden turn in the road forced the truck to maneuver a tight corner.

"Hey! Watch out!" shouted bystanders on the sidewalk. As the truck turned, Douglas passed right over their heads, barely missing the glass window of the First National Bank.

"That was a close call!" Douglas said to himself. The trucks drove through town and back onto the main highway, until they reached another sign:

Welcome to Silver Star. Population 30.

The trucks pulled into what appeared to be a junkyard. As they parked, a pleasant-faced woman emerged from a small house and stood on the porch looking at Douglas.

"Lloyd Harkins, what in the world have you got there?"

"It's a near perfect beam from the old Bell Diamond Mine," Lloyd called back to his wife. "They don't make 'em like this anymore, Anne. This old beam is over 90 feet long!"

For years, Lloyd's wife had seen him haul all kinds of old relics home. "You know, Lloyd," she shouted, "if the Egyptian pyramids were closer, you'd probably try to drag one of those home, too!" Lloyd didn't hear her, because he was already thinking that Douglas would look nice near the highway, in front of his old locomotive and refurbished caboose.

Lloyd Harkins knew a lot about the 3 Rs: reduce, reuse, and recycle. He operated a salvage company, where he rescued and restored old machinery.

From time to time, Lloyd loaned or sold some of his industrial equipment. Once, the Smithsonian Institute borrowed his prized Panama Canal steam shovel for a year. The Walt Disney Company bought old mining equipment to model their Gold Rush roller coaster at Frontier Land, Thunder Mountain and for the Indiana Jones rides at Disneyland Tokyo. To his wife's chagrin, the objects that Lloyd couldn't sell or trade ended up on display in their front yard. People driving past the town of Silver Star on Route 41 were greeted by the remarkable sight of Lloyd's many curiosities.

But would Douglas ever be more than a roadside attraction?

Douglas is
DISCOVERED AT LAST

Thirty-four years later, in 1999, a blue truck stopped outside Lloyd Harkins's house.

The driver got out and stood staring at Douglas through the chain-link fence. He walked toward the house and knocked on the door.

"Hi there," the visitor said, as Lloyd opened the front door. "I was driving by and saw that big beam along the side of the road. I wonder if you'd consider selling it? I have a company that reuses old timber in new buildings."

"He's a beauty, isn't he?" replied Lloyd. "I've become pretty attached to him, but I'd consider selling him for the right price."

The men walked down the front porch steps and toward Douglas. They walked slowly around his enormous length, discussing his value and eventually settling on a price. "One problem," the visitor said. "It'll be awhile before I can pick him up."

"That's no problem," Lloyd responded with a smile. "He's not going to run away! We're happy to have him here until you can come and get him."

Eighteen months later, on a frigid February morning, an 18-wheeler truck pulled two flatbeds up to Lloyd's house to begin Douglas's journey home.

A crane lifted him into the air and laid him onto the flatbeds. Once each end was securely tied down, the truck pulled out of the yard. Anne and Lloyd waved from their front porch as Douglas left his home of 36 years.

The truck turned onto a major highway and headed west toward Washington State and the Cascade Mountains. Ten hours later, the truck shifted into its lowest gear to begin the long climb up to Snoqualmie Pass, where it was snowing, and the fragrant scent of the evergreen forest filled the frosty air around him.

As they passed over the summit and headed down the west side of the mountains, the snow turned to rain. Douglas was back in familiar territory, yet things had changed dramatically since he had left more than 100 years ago. The old highway was lined with buildings and signs.

But one thing had not changed. When the truck crossed the long, low bridge over Lake Washington, the familiar snow-covered peak of Mount Rainier stood to the south.

It was as if his favorite mountain was welcoming him back.

The truck maneuvered through downtown Seattle to the waterfront and pulled into a dock named Pier 91. As a crane lifted Douglas off the truck and onto the dock, seagulls circled above and called as if asking, "Where are you going?"

A week later, in the early morning, a small group of people gathered on the dock next to Douglas.

Awaiting the arrival of a special scale, Douglas was about to be weighed. If he weighed less than 9,000 pounds, Columbia Helicopters had agreed to airlift him to his destination. He had weighed over 10,000 pounds when he was milled more than 100 years ago. Had he grown heavier or lighter over the last century?

"Please step back folks! Here comes the scale!" hollered the man in charge. They weighed one end of Douglas, then the other. People placed their bets on the final number while the machine calculated the total weight.

"This beam weighs 8,864 pounds!" bellowed the man next to the scale.

The announcement brought a loud cheer from the spectators. Douglas had lost over 1,000 pounds because he no longer contained all the water he had absorbed while his roots were deep in the ground.

A few days later, on Valentine's Day, a large helicopter arrived at the dock. It hovered above Douglas, creating strong wind currents below. Its crew lowered heavy steel cables to the pier. A team of men rushed forward to secure the cables around Douglas, then stepped back as he was slowly lifted into the air.

Douglas was flying above Puget Sound, just like his friends the eagles.

The helicopter headed west toward Bainbridge Island and Blakely Harbor, where Douglas had grown up. Cormorants with outstretched wings stood on the large rock that sat just beyond the harbor, while a welcoming committee of seals bobbed their heads out of the water.

Life around the harbor had changed since Douglas had left more than 100 years ago. The mill was gone and, once again, a thick green forest covered the hills where he had flourished for centuries. Many of his children had grown to heights of 150 feet, and his old forest community looked healthy and strong.

The helicopter turned north and flew up the hillside to a small clearing in the trees. As it slowed and hovered above, Douglas was lowered to some workmen in hard hats who had been waiting for him. When the giant beam reached the ground, they untied him and gave a thumbs-up to the helicopter, which rose and quickly flew off.

With all eyes on Douglas, a crowd of several dozen people broke into hearty cheers and applause.

The Tree
THAT CAME HOME

Douglas had arrived at a construction site very close to where he had begun his life 300 years ago. An outdoor education center called IslandWood was being built for children to explore the land and learn about the history of the place where he grew up. Douglas had an important new purpose: He was to be part of the lessons!

The next day, a beautiful cedar carving was lifted into place at the site. The woven cedar dress on the carving reminded him of his old friend Skukuoy. Soon children and adults began gathering for what appeared to be a special ceremony. A woman stood on the bare cement foundation of one of the buildings under construction.

"We have two treasures to welcome here today!" she announced proudly.

Walking toward the cedar carving, she said, "The cedar pole being raised today was carved to honor a Native American elder, Vi Hilbert, who has spent her life preserving our native traditions. The carving will welcome children and help us share stories about the First People who originally inhabited this land."

Turning in the other direction, the woman pointed to Douglas. "This giant 92-foot beam will become the centerpiece of our school's primary building, representing a permanent monument to the mill town that operated near this site over 100 years ago."

"I've never seen a piece of timber that big in my entire life!" one man exclaimed.

A young boy's eyes grew wide as he gazed at Douglas. Turning to his little sister, he whispered, "That would make the biggest teeter-totter in the world!"

Architects were already at work designing a special ceiling truss where Douglas's extraordinary length could be displayed between the school's two giant rooms.

On the morning of February 28, 2001, a crane lifted him into his permanent home.

Two workmen, suspended in mid-air, were bolting Douglas to the truss when, suddenly, an earthquake hit. It was a whopper, measuring 6.8 on the Richter Scale. The earth's tremendous tremors rocked the workmen inside the bucket of the crane, while the people standing below watched nervously.

To Douglas, the quake seemed like an appropriate welcome home. After all, it was the great quake of 1700 that had provided the perfect clearing in which he could begin his life.

When the tremor ended, the workmen finished securing Douglas into place. One end pointed directly at the large cedar carving so reminiscent of Skukuoy. The other end extended into the room where he would welcome visitors to this new school in the woods.

That summer, a Seattle artist named Buster Simpson took the ferry to visit Douglas.

He had created an impressive metal sculpture that would wrap around one end of Douglas in the school's Welcome Center. For six hours, the artist worked to attach wires to the ceiling so that he could suspend a 40-foot band saw blade around Douglas—just like a Möbius strip. Hand painted on the blade was a quote that echoed the words of the conservationist John Muir—and a lesson Douglas had learned from his parent so long ago:

Tug on anything and you will find
it connected to everything else.

IslandWood officially opened its doors to students on September 21, 2002.

That Monday morning, eager fourth and fifth graders arrived at the school in the woods, where they would spend the week learning about the land where Douglas had grown up. After the students unpacked and got settled in their lodges, an instructor led a small group of them into one of the large rooms that Douglas occupied.

"Wow! That beam is awesome!" shouted one student.

"It must have come from the biggest tree in the world!" exclaimed another.

"How did it get here?" one boy asked.

Soon they all wanted to hear the story of "the tree that came home."

Now more than 300 years old ...

and less than a mile from where he grew up, Douglas greets thousands of students each year.

They come to IslandWood to experience the wonders of the natural world.

At the end of the week, students return home with a gift from Douglas—a message that has been passed down through many generations of trees:

"We are all interconnected, and each one of us has a unique gift to contribute to the world around us."

Additional Resources

1700 The great quake occurs in January and Douglas's seed falls to the ground.

1712 Douglas's parent tree falls and becomes a nurse log.

1762 Douglas meets and develops a friendship with Skukuoy.

1767 Drought – Douglas hardly grows at all.

1776 America declares independence from British rule.

1792 Captain Vancouver visits Restoration Point and Blakely Harbor.

1841 Captain Charles Wilkes surveys the waters of the Northwest and names Bainbridge Island and Blakely Harbor.

Growth rings of the Douglas-fir tree

Historical Dates

■ History of Douglas

■ Important dates in our history

1851 First Euro-Americans arrive at Alki Point, founding Seattle.

1853 Henry Yesler's sawmill is built in Seattle.

1862 First public education classes in Seattle.

1863 Captain Renton tests the depth of Blakely Harbor on Bainbridge Island.

1864 Port Blakely Mill is built in Blakely Harbor.

1865 U.S. Civil War begins.

1880 Hall Brothers Shipyard built in Blakely Harbor.

1888 Fire destroys the first Port Blakely Sawmill.

1889 Washington becomes the 42nd state. The great Seattle fire burns over 25 city blocks.

1900 Douglas is logged and taken to the Bell Diamond Mine in Montana.

1907 A second fire occurs at Port Blakely Mill.

1922 Port Blakely Mill closes, never reopens.

1929 U.S. stock market crashes – the Great Depression follows.

1930 Bell Diamond Mine in Montana closes.

1939 World War II begins.

1962 Seattle World's Fair opens.

1965 Douglas moves to Lloyd Harkins's home in Silver Star, Montana.

1998 255 acres purchased to create IslandWood, a school in the woods.

1999 Gary Engman purchases and donates Douglas to IslandWood.

2001 Douglas flies by helicopter to Bainbridge Island on February 14. Earthquake hits February 28.

2002 IslandWood opens on September 21.

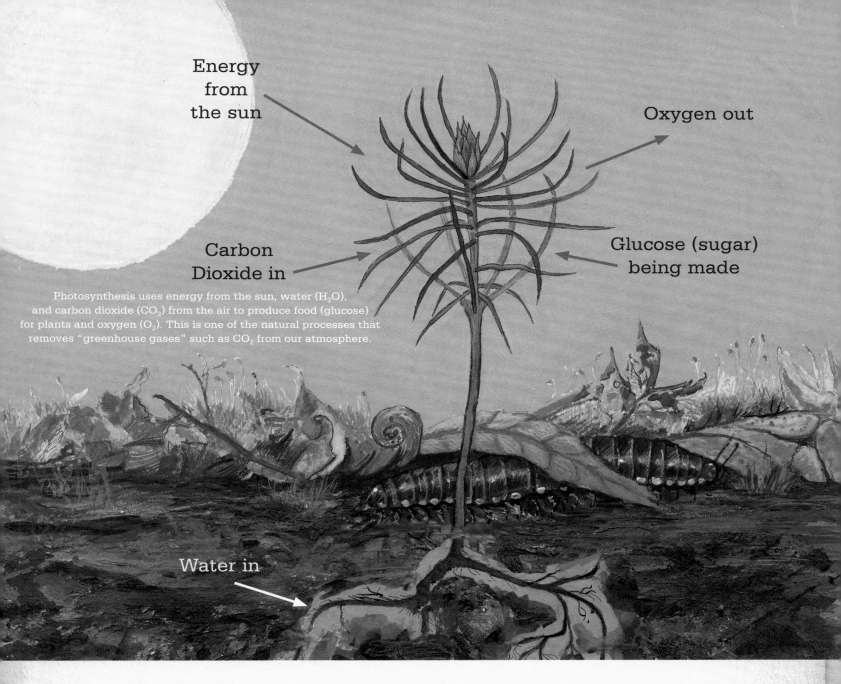

Energy
from
the sun

Oxygen out

Carbon
Dioxide in

Glucose (sugar)
being made

Photosynthesis uses energy from the sun, water (H_2O),
and carbon dioxide (CO_2) from the air to produce food (glucose)
for plants and oxygen (O_2). This is one of the natural processes that
removes "greenhouse gases" such as CO_2 from our atmosphere.

Water in

Photosynthesis

Photosynthesis is a chemical process plants perform with the sun to produce energy (sugar).
Plant leaves (or needles) have cells called chloroplasts which contain a green pigment called
chlorophyll. The chlorophyll enables photosynthesis to occur and it gives plants their green color.

Chemical Equation:

$$6\ H_2O + 6\ CO_2 \longrightarrow C_6H_{12}O_6 + 6\ O_2$$

Plants are often called the "Lungs of the Earth" because they absorb carbon dioxide and give
off oxygen. This is the reverse of animals and humans, who inhale oxygen and exhale carbon
dioxide. We all depend on photosynthesis for our food and oxygen.

A Douglas-fir Tree Develops 3 Types of Buds

Pollen Cone Buds

These buds produce the pollen that fertilizes the seeds. Pollen cones shed dust-like powder (pollen), which is transferred by wind to the female cones on another tree.

Vegetative Buds

These buds develop into needles which stay on the tree for two to three years. A mature tree can have 65 million needles.

Seed Cone Buds

When these buds are fertilized by pollen from another tree, they develop into large mature cones. These cones produce the seeds that ripen in autumn and are scattered by wind and gravity.

The position of a bud on a branch helps determine which type of bud it will develop into.

Pollen cone bud
develops near the point of attachment to the branch

Vegetative bud
develops at the end of the branch

Seed cone bud
develops along the shoot of the branch

Mature cone
is the result of a seed cone that was fertilized by the pollen of another tree

Did You Know?

- Each mature tree (80-plus years old) produces about 800 cones annually.

- Each cone produces between 25 and 50 seeds, and an average mature tree can produce one pound of seed—or 40,000 seeds—per crop!

- The chance of a seed developing into a mature tree is only one in 1,000.

- Only one in 100,000 seeds survives to become a mature, old-growth tree!

GERMINATION OF A CONIFER SEED

The Wing helps to disperse seed by wind and gravity

Seed

[1] The Seed

In the fall, cones mature and seeds fall to the ground. Douglas squirrels harvest the seeds and store them for winter. Mice, voles, insects and birds also extract the seeds from the cones for food. The seeds that survive on the ground remain dormant through the winter and wait for favorable conditions to grow in the spring.

[2] Germination begins

In spring the seed begins to absorb moisture from the earth and to swell. The root tip inside the seed splits the outer covering of the seed coat and begins to extend outside the seed. The seeds grow best in exposed mineral soil, so they are often found in areas where past disturbances, such as fire, have opened the forest to sunlight.

[3] Root (radicle) emerges

Enough fuel (nutrients) is stored in the seed to power the root to extend, elongate and push out of the seed coat. Gravity guides it downward as it buries its tip in the earth. The root begins to anchor the seed. Now the root will supplement the seed's internal supply of energy for the next stage of development.

[4] Seed leaves (cotyledons) emerge

The root reaches down into the soil to take in additional moisture and nutrients for the seed leaves or needles, which are fully developed inside the seed coat. As the leaves or needles swell, they emerge outside the seed and stretch toward the light.

[5] Photosynthesis begins

The final stage of germination is reached when the stem of the seedling straightens and the seed leaves or needles start to exit the shell, fan out and begin photosynthesis. The seed coat then falls to the ground having completed its job of protecting the seed during its dormancy and germination.

[6] Growth continues

After photosynthesis begins the seedling is able to support further growth. The seedlings will grow 2 1/2 to 3 1/2 inches during their first year. They grow best in light shade in the beginning of their life but need more sun as they grow older.

Pacific Northwest Conifers

		Age	Diameter	Height
Douglas-fir	Typical:	>750 years	5 - 7 feet	230 - 262 feet
	Maximum:	1,300 years	14.4 feet	328 feet

Most Popular Use: As the most important tree in the west, it produces valuable lumber for homes and shipbuilding and is used for plywood and fuel. This fast-growing tree is a prized Christmas tree and is often used for reforestation.

		Age	Diameter	Height
Grand Fir	Typical:	>400 years	3 - 5 feet	148 - 197 feet
	Maximum:	>500? years	6.6 feet	266 feet

Most Popular Use: Less common than the Douglas-fir (and sometimes difficult to grow), it is a prized ornamental tree and is also harvested as a Christmas tree.

		Age	Diameter	Height
Western Redcedar	Typical:	>1,000 years	5 - 10 feet	131 - 164 feet
	Maximum:	1,400(>2,000?) years	20.7 feet	233 feet

Most Popular Use: Important for outside lumber and furniture (rot-resistant) and for wooden shingles and shakes. Also used extensively for poles, fence posts and boat building. Its inner bark continues to be used in basket making.

		Age	Diameter	Height
Western Hemlock	Typical:	>500 years	3 - 4 feet	164 - 213 feet
	Maximum:	1,238 years	9 feet	246 feet

Most Popular Use: Easy to carve and used for lumber production, in pulpwood, and in making paper and fiberboard.

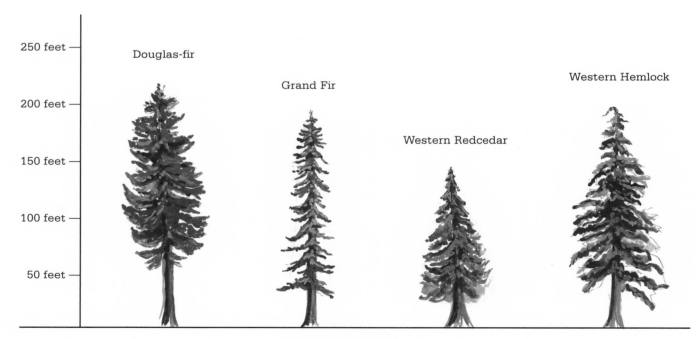

250 feet — Douglas-fir

Grand Fir

200 feet —

Western Hemlock

Western Redcedar

150 feet —

100 feet —

50 feet —

400 years old

Douglas-fir

Likes moist forests with well-drained soils. Grows best in sunlight. Thick bark (can be 14") with conical crown and spreading branches that are uniformly spaced.

Key Characteristics: Cones have three-forked bracts extending beyond the scales; it looks like mice are hiding in the cones with their hind feet and tail showing.

three-forked bracts

Grand Fir

Grows under the canopy of Douglas-firs in dry to moist conifer forests (in rain shadow areas). Thin bark with dense branches.

Key Characteristics: Needles lie on a horizontal plane giving the branches a flat appearance (dark green on top, whitish color underneath).

Western Redcedar

Likes wet, rich soils (moist to swampy). Grows well in shaded forests or near rivers and streams. Bark is thin and tears off in long fibrous strips.

Key Characteristics: Branches droop slightly and turn up into a "J" shape.

Western Hemlock

Most shade-tolerant of all conifers in our region. Seedlings often grow on nurse logs, and can grow in fairly dry to wet sites. Thick bark with delicate, graceful downsweeping branches.

Key Characteristics: The very top branch is typically bent like a whip.

Real People, Places & Things

You have met in The Tree that Came Home

Bainbridge Island – a city in Washington State and an island in Puget Sound. In 1841, U.S. Navy Lieutenant Charles Wilkes visited the island while surveying the Northwest. Lt. Wilkes named the island after Commodore William Bainbridge, the commander of the frigate *Constitution* in the War of 1812. Bainbridge Island was originally a center for the logging and shipbuilding industries. The island was known for its huge, accessible cedar trees, which were especially in demand for the building of ships' masts.

Bell Diamond Mine – a mine built around 1890 near Butte, Montana, which originally mined gold, then silver and finally copper. (It never mined diamonds.) It ceased operation in the early 1930s.

Blakely Rock – a large outcropping of rock off the mouth of Blakely Harbor on Bainbridge Island. It was named for Captain Johnston Blakely, an American hero in the War of 1812.

Captain George Vancouver – led an expedition to the North Pacific in search of scientific and commercial information for the British government. He arrived in Puget Sound on the ship *Discovery* in April of 1792 to begin his exploration. The following month, he anchored off Bainbridge Island and proceeded to survey the waters and name many of the islands, mountains, waterways and points of land in sight.

Captain William Renton – a sea captain as well as a lumber and shipping merchant, founded Port Blakely Mill Company, one of several lumber mills he started in Puget Sound. In 1863, he found the depth of Blakely Harbor to be deep enough for oceangoing ships. Over the next year he purchased over 400 acres surrounding the harbor to build the sawmill and town.

Columbia Helicopters – one of the world's largest heavy-lift helicopter companies, which provided a twin-bladed Boeing Vertol helicopter to airlift the beam from Pier 91 in Seattle to IslandWood's construction site on Bainbridge Island.

Eagle – a large bird, 35 to 40 inches tall, with a wingspan of up to 6 1/2 feet. Eagles spend much of their day perched high in trees overlooking bays. Even though they are fish eaters, they will take ducks and birds or whatever prey is available and easiest to obtain. In the Native American culture, the bald eagle is a symbol of strength, endurance and vision. It is often considered the protector and carrier of prayers and the connection to the Spirit/Soul/Creator.

Earthquake – a strong shaking or disturbance of the earth's surface caused by sudden underground movement. About 1,000 years ago, a giant earthquake struck Puget Sound. One result was the creation of the point of land south of Blakely Harbor (Restoration Point) on Bainbridge Island. The area was suddenly thrust up 21 feet. The Nisqually earthquake of February 28, 2001 was a magnitude of 6.8. Damage was reported in the Seattle area, but there were no fatalities. During the earthquake, IslandWood's giant Douglas-fir beam was still on the scaffolding as workmen made final adjustments to its installation at the ridge of the Great Hall. The men quickly climbed down. The beam was not affected.

First People (see Suquamish, next page) – also known as Native Americans, American Indians or native people; the people whose ancestors lived in North America before the Europeans arrived.

Great Horned Owl – is probably best known for the large tufts of feathers on its head that look like horns. It is about 24 inches tall, with a wingspan of more than 4 feet. It has big cat-like eyes; its brown white, gray, and black markings look like the bark of a tree, which help camouflage it in the woods. These owls hunt for prey at night, catching and eating mammals, fish and birds.

House Post – carved from a cedar log, these posts often stood at both ends of the longhouse (a structure built by the First People and housing many families under one roof). Many of these posts had carved and painted family crest figures. At IslandWood, the house post standing at one end of the Great Hall was carved from a 20-foot redcedar harvested from a Haida site on the Prince of Wales Island, Alaska. It was carved by First People Roger Fernandes, Lower Elwa Klallam, and Bruce Cook, Haida. The outstretched arms represent the welcoming arms of a grandmother to visiting children and honor Vi Hilbert, Upper Skagit Elder. Peg Deam wove the figure's cape and skirt from redcedar inner bark.

Lloyd Harkins – with his wife Anne, runs a seven-acre salvage company (objects rescued for reuse) in Silver Star, Montana. Harkins, a former copper miner, searches for historical objects that might otherwise disintegrate or be lost.

Mithūn Architects – the Seattle architectural firm that designed the IslandWood campus and integrated Douglas's beam as a special feature of the Great Hall and Welcome Center.

Pileated Woodpecker – is one of the largest woodpeckers found in North America—about 15 inches in length. It eats insects, fruits and nuts; a large part of its diet consists of carpenter ants and beetle larvae. It uses its sharp bill to pull bark off trees and expose ant colonies. It extracts the ants with its long sticky tongue. It also uses its long bill to dig large rectangular holes in trees to create roosting and nesting spots.

Port Blakely Mill – a sawmill built in 1864 on the southeast side of Bainbridge Island. Captain Renton purchased the land around Port Blakely Harbor because the harbor was deep enough for sailing ships to come and go. The sheltered waters were also perfect for storing large log rafts to supply the mill. During the next four decades, The Port Blakely Mill Company became the world's largest sawmill under one roof. Its lumber was shipped all over the world. The mill burned down in February of 1888. It was rebuilt only to be destroyed by a second fire in 1907. The Port Blakely mill was once again rebuilt but on a smaller scale. It closed in 1922 and was dismantled in 1924.

Port Blakely toothpick – a term used to describe very long Douglas-fir tree beams that were produced at the Port Blakely Mill. This was the largest lumber mill in the world in the late 1800s. The mill had a reputation for cutting bigger, longer beams than any other mill in the world. It took two railroad flatcars to hold them.

Puget Sound – an arm of the Pacific Ocean in northwestern Washington State. George Vancouver named it after Peter Puget, who was a lieutenant in his expedition and explored the southern end of Puget Sound in May of 1792.

Smithsonian Institute – the world's largest museum complex, located in Washington D.C. It was established to connect us to our history and our heritage as Americans and to promote innovation, research and discovery in science.

Suquamish – a southern Coast Salish Native American people who spoke a dialect of Lushootseed. The Suquamish relied on fishing from local rivers and Puget Sound for their food, and built plank longhouses to protect themselves from the wet winters west of the Cascade Mountains. During the spring and fall, the Suquamish traveled by canoes throughout the Puget Sound region gathering food, medicine, and materials for baskets and clothing.

Vi Hilbert – a revered Upper Skagit Elder who has dedicated her life to perpetuating her tribe's language and traditions. Vi is a linguist, educator and storyteller. She has devoted much time to the study, promotion and preservation of her childhood language, Lushootseed Salish, and the oral literature and culture of her people. In 2006, Vi donated a collection of native baskets to IslandWood to help teach children about the native people. She believes the baskets have stories to tell if you hold them quietly; they speak to you through the materials, designs and spirits of those who wove them.

Glossary

Words worth knowing from The Tree that Came Home

Abiotic – non-living (never having been of life) parts of an ecosystem.

Artifact – an object remaining from a particular period of time in human history.

Biotic – living things, including anything caused and produced by a living thing.

Bract – a modified leaf, either small and scale-like or large and pedal-like.

Branch – a woody stem growing from the trunk of a tree or the main stem of a plant.

Buckers – men who took the limbs off of fallen trees and sawed the trees into logs.

Bullwhackers – men who drove the teams of bull oxen that dragged the logs to the water or to a cliff that led to the water. These men used a whip, called a bull-whack, to make the oxen move.

Canopy – the leafy cover formed by the upper branches of trees in a forest.

Circumference – the distance around a circle.

Conifer tree – evergreen, cone-bearing tree or shrub, normally with needles for leaves.

Crosscut saw – long, two-handled saw used by two men to cut through the trunks of large trees.

Crown – the upper part of a tree, including the branches and foliage.

Cycle – a periodically repeated sequence of events.

Deciduous tree – a tree that loses leaves annually in autumn and grows new leaves in the spring.

Decompose – the breakdown of organic matter; decay.

Disintegrate – to break into small parts.

Drought – an extended period with no rain.

Duff – plant debris in various stages of rot on the forest floor that eventually becomes soil.

Ecosystem – an interconnected complex of plant and animal communities and their associated biotic and abiotic environment.

Estuary – the lower part of a river where it nears the sea and the tide flows in, causing fresh and salt water to mix.

Evaporate – the process of a liquid turning into a vapor as a result of being heated or exposed to air.

Evergreen – plants that have green leaves or needles for the entire year.

Fallers – men who cut down the trees.

Fertile – refers to rich soil that is capable of sustaining abundant growth.

Fertilize – in soil, the process of adding a substance to provide additional nutrients for plants. In flowers or cones, the transfer of pollen from the male to the female.

Flourish – to grow stronger and prosper.

Furl – to fold or roll (a sail).

Germination – the process of starting to grow following pollination or fertilization.

Growth rings – a layer of wood cells added to a tree trunk or stem during one growing season that can be seen in a horizontal cross-section cut through the trunk. Each ring marks one year; its size and width depend on weather, growing conditions and random events (such as fire or drought).

Habitat – a place or environment where a plant or animal lives and grows naturally.

Harbor – a sheltered body of water that is a safe place for boats or ships to dock or rest away from strong winds.

Headframe – a framework that is constructed over the top of a mineshaft; it supports the pulleys that raise and lower the lift used to transport materials and workers into and out of the mine.

Inhabit – to dwell or live in; to occupy.

Interconnected – a state of being joined or linked together.

Landscapes – an expanse of scenery that can be seen in a single view.

Larvae – the first major mobile life stage of an insect or first development following egg hatching.

Migrating – the act of moving to a new area when the seasons change, or for the purposes of finding food or mates; birds often migrate.

Möbius strip – a continuous closed surface or band; formed from a rectangular strip by rotating one end 180 degrees and joining it with the other end.

Nourishment – food or other substances necessary for life and growth.

Nurse log – a decaying stump or log on which plants, such as moss, ferns, berry bushes and trees grow, nursed by the nutrients in the decomposing (rotting) wood.

Nutrients – in nature, the food from the soil or other organic materials that supports and aids plant growth.

Ore – a rock containing a metal that is valuable enough to be mined, such as copper, silver or gold.

Photosynthesis – a chemical process plants perform with the sun to produce energy (sugar). *See page 48 for more details.*

Pitch – a sticky organic substance or resin discharged from the bark of various conifer trees.

Predator – an animal that hunts other animals for food.

Raucous – unpleasantly loud and harsh.

Recycle – to use discarded material for another purpose, minimizing waste.

Relic – an object that is interesting because of its old age or associations.

Rigging – the general term for all of the lines, ropes, wires, and chains on a vessel or ship.

Rupturing – the state of being torn open or of bursting.

Salmonberries – a shrub with reddish-orange berries related to the raspberry and blackberry.

Sapling – a young tree that has developed sap, the vital fluid that circulates inside a woody plant.

Seedling – a plant or tree grown from a seed, in its early stages of development.

Spawn – fish reproduction; breeding by releasing eggs and sperm into the water.

Spawning ground – the area where fish come to release their eggs and sperm into the water.

Springboard – a board that was intersected into notches on opposite sides of a large tree trunk where lumberjacks stood to use their cross-cut saw.

Transformation – change from one form to another.

Tremor – shaking movement.

Truss – a rigid, jointed structure usually in a triangular pattern that supports long spans in a roof.

Unfurled – to unfold or unroll (a sail).

Watershed – an area of land that drains into a particular body of water.

Weave – the manner in which a basket is formed by interlacing materials, such as inner cedar bark.

Web of life – interactions and connections between all living and non-living things in our world.

Wharf – a structure built out over the water where boats can dock and load or unload cargo.

Winching – an electrical or motorized device used to wind ropes in lifting heavy cargo.

Chapter Discussion Questions

The Night the Earth Shook

1. What changes did the earthquake in 1700 cause?
2. How did the earthquake's devastation create the potential for new life?
3. How was the bark of the Douglas-fir tree different from the other trees' bark?
4. Why were there big forest fires in the summer after the earthquake?
5. How did the forest ecosystem change in the months and years right after the earthquake?
6. Can you imagine other changes that are not mentioned in the story?
7. How do forest animals protect themselves and each other from predators?
8. How do natural processes work to ensure seeds get to the ground where they can grow? What might stop this from happening?
9. What factors contribute to a seed's chances for survival from seedling to mature tree? List some that are abiotic, biotic and cultural.
10. What does the process of photosynthesis need in order to produce energy (or sugar) for all plants and trees?
11. What are some things that might make it difficult for saplings or very young trees to survive?
12. How are big storms like the one Douglas experienced in his sixth year important to the forest ecosystem? How do storms contribute to forest succession?

The Web of Life

1. What are some of the things that might shorten the life of an older or more mature tree?
2. Describe a mutually beneficial relationship between a tree and a bird.
3. What is meant by the "web of life"?
4. How are things in the forest interconnected? What are some examples?
5. How does the parent tree fit into forest succession? How does this keep the forest ecosystem healthy?
6. What connections do you have with trees like Douglas and his parent? What other plants are connected to you or your family's life?

A Girl Named Skukuoy

1. How are the Suquamish people interconnected with the forest?
2. Skukuoy and Douglas become friends. What friendships do you have with other species of life?
3. What are some of the ways the Suquamish people use cedar trees? Fir trees?
4. How do the Suquamish people teach their children life skills?
5. Skukuoy was eager to make water-tight baskets. What do you look forward to learning?
6. What do you think is meant by "true friendship"? Why are friends important to have?
7. What impact does a drought have on the forest? Describe its impact in terms of the concept of interconnectedness.
8. Why do you think Skukuoy's family always visits Douglas's environment?

The Arrival of Ships & Settlers

1. Why were the explorers visiting new parts of the world?
2. Compare and contrast the Suquamish people's relationship to the land to that of the new settlers.
3. What was Captain Renton doing with the rope and hunk of iron?
4. How do you think Skukuoy's people felt when they saw the new mill town of Port Blakely in 1863? What do you think they did next?

The Age of Fallers, Buckers & Bullwhackers

1. How did the Port Blakely mill town change the natural environment of the harbor?
2. How did Bainbridge Island change with the rising of the mills and Port Blakely?
3. What do you think life was like for the children who grew up at Port Blakely?
4. How did the lumberjacks determine the diameter of Douglas? What do you think was the mathematical equation they used?
5. Why did the fallers chop a V-shaped wedge into Douglas?

Douglas Leaves Home

1. Compare the ecosystems of Blakely harbor on Bainbridge Island where Douglas grew up to that of Butte, Montana.
2. Can you think of ways Douglas could potentially be used?
3. How might the Montana weather affect Douglas?
4. How could Lloyd's collecting of old machines and large equipment help serve a purpose in our world?
5. How is Lloyd's work important?

Douglas is Discovered at Last

1. How had Puget Sound changed in the 100 years or so that Douglas had been away? In what ways was it almost the same?
2. How do you think it feels to go home after a long absence? What changes more— you or home?
3. Why do you think the helicopter would only airlift Douglas if he weighed less than 9,000 pounds?
4. Why do cormorants seem to be one of the only birds that sit with their wings outstretched?
5. How did Douglas lose so much weight?

The Tree that Came Home

1. Do you think that teaching children about the land and its First People makes a difference in the world? Why?
2. If Douglas and the House Post had a conversation, what do you think they would say?
3. What is a Möbius strip?
4. What does the sculpture around Douglas symbolize?
5. What connections seem most interesting or important in this story? In the ecosystems of IslandWood?
6. How does "having a purpose" seem important to you?

Special Thanks
From Debbi Brainerd

I'm afraid *The Tree that Came Home* would have never come home (in textbook form), had it not been for **Linda Strickler**. Linda's gentle prodding kept me moving forward toward each new phase of the book. I will always treasure the laughs we shared, dealing with the challenges the book presented along the way.

My thanks to **Kathleen Maynard** for coming up with the book title that inspired me to write the story.

I am grateful to the following people, who made it possible for Douglas to come back home:

- **Lloyd Harkins** for discovering the beam at the Silver Star mine and hauling it to his Montana residence/business.
- **Gary Engman** for locating the beam at Lloyd Harkins's place and donating it to IslandWood.
- **Dana Warren** for figuring out a game plan for returning the beam to Bainbridge Island.
- **Columbia Helicopters** for flying the beam "gratis" from the Port of Seattle across Puget Sound to IslandWood.
- **Dave Goldberg, Rich Franko** and **Bert Gregory** for integrating the beam into IslandWood's architectural design.

Thanks to those who helped me in the creation of the book:

Barbara Winther, Vi Hilmo, Katherine Zecca, Karen Ferguson, Linda Strickler, Virginia Hand and **Scott Clark.**

Much appreciation to those who provided invaluable feedback and edits along the way:

Catherine Allchin, Karin Beck, Sally Black, Jabe Blumenthal, Allyson Brown, Ray Cramer, Dee Dickinson, Jennifer Dixon, Jane Douglas, Denise Dumouchel, Gregory Glynn, Caryl Grosch, Judy Harris, Jan Jackson, Katie Jennings, Ben Klasky, Marjorie Lamarre, Rex Lybrand, Mary Ann Mackin, Fred Moody, Beth Morgan, Liza Nagel, Andrew Price, Cheryl Ross, Karen Salsbury, Katherine James Schuitemaker, Doug Sprugel, Alison Swain, Jack Swanson, Melinda West, and **Clancy Wolf.**

When it seemed as though we would never complete the project, fate and good fortune sent us book designer, **Nancy Stumvoll**, and editor, **Karen Wilson**, who transformed our text and illustrations into a real book.

Finally, we are especially grateful to ...

West Coast Paper, Domtar and **ColorGraphics**, whose generous contributions helped make it possible for thousands of copies of *The Tree that Came Home* to be given to children and teachers in classrooms across the Puget Sound region.